Table of Contents

Prologue: The Accident.....................................4
Chapter 1: The Nobody..................................11
Chapter 2: The Flight.......................................19
Chapter 3: The Happy Place..........................25
Chapter 4: The House.....................................33
Chapter 5: The Rebel......................................39
Chapter 6: The Helper....................................67
Chapter 7: The Reflection..............................82
Chapter 8: The Visitor....................................99
Chapter 9: The Mother.................................112
Chapter 10: The Fade....................................116
Chapter 11: The Promise..............................127
Chapter 12: The Escape................................129
Chapter 13: Epilogue.....................................135

Prologue:

The Accident.

"Okay, one last push Janie, and then I have to go!"

Mike had a good life. He worked hard every day as a construction worker and provided well for his family. His wife, Sheryl, was the perfect woman; beautiful, funny, kind, and the best mom in the world.

Life was good.

Mike was at the park with his 5-year-old daughter, Jane, pushing her on the swing set, when his cell phone rang.

"It's my boss… I have to take it. Hold on, sweetie." Mike gave Jane one last strong push on the swing and stepped away to check his phone.

He's going to kill me. I'm late for my shift, and he's going to kill me, I just know it. He glanced anxiously at Jane before answering the phone.

"You better get your ass into work right now, Mike, I swear to god." Mike's boss, Leslie, always seemed like he had a stick up his... you know where. Mike wondered if it was because he had a girl's name as a contractor for a construction company. Either way, he knew he had to cut his time with his precious daughter short and get into work before he got fired.

"Baby girl, I'm sorry, but we have to go home. Daddy has to go to work." He looked at his daughter's pleading eyes as she whined to him, begging him to stay at the park. Mike sighed.

Mike and his daughter Jane had the perfect father-daughter relationship, the type you'd see in commercials on the TV for coffee or insurance or something else. When Mike wasn't working, he was playing with Jane. They'd go on long walks together in the park, go to the movies together to watch silly cartoon movies, read books together, and do anything else you can imagine. He loved his daughter.

Mike also loved his wife, Sheryl, dearly. She was the mother to his precious Janie, of course, so how could he not? He had met Sheryl when they were in high school when she was a cheerleader and he was a linebacker on the football team. They had a beautiful relationship over the years full of fun, taking lots of drives down to Fredericksburg on long weekends to go hiking and tour the wineries. In their 10 years together, they never fought once. Even when Sheryl was pregnant with Jane, and she was puking every day, they never argued or spat about anything at all. *I'm so thankful for my girls,* Mike thought to himself.

Mike, like all of his peers on his small-town high school football team, did not go into football for college. Mike decided after high school instead of going to college to work for the construction company down the street because the money was good and they were hiring. It wasn't fulfilling work, but it paid well and it was steady enough. It provided enough that Sheryl didn't have to work, at least, and could stay home with their perfect daughter. Anything was worth their happiness to Mike.

Despite Jane's protests, he picks up her daughter off the swingset, careful not to scrape her shins against the child-size swing. They were heading home and he had to leave his family behind for the day, but he was comforted knowing that he would be coming home to them that evening.

~

"You're going to be late, hun!" Sheryl called from the kitchen over a sink of dirty dishes. "I know, babe, I'm going, I'm going. Just had to put Jane down in her room for a nap." Mike yelled back from outside of Jane's door.

He tip-toed through the living room of their modest home and snuck up behind Sheryl before swooping her in his arms, just like on their wedding day. She squealed in delight. "Oh hun, stop it!" She playfully slapped his arm. "Seriously, you're going to be late, and I don't think Ashley, or Larry, or whatever his name is, is going to be happy." Mike put her down, while she held her head in her hands. "You can't lose this job, baby. Things are hard enough as it is, and if you didn't have your job, and with me not working..."

"It's Leslie, and don't you worry about that. Things are perfect. I'm not going to lose my job, and we have everything we need! I have you and Jane, and a house, and whatever that is cooking in the crockpot over there..." Mike smirked at his wife. He knew just how to make her feel better.

"Okay, if you say so. Now you better get going! Dinner will be ready when you get back." she replied with a look of relief on her face. "Shredded pork tacos!"

"Can't wait. Love you." Mike said to Sheryl.

"Love you too."

~

It was when Sheryl noticed that Mike wasn't home yet and his shift had ended an hour beforehand when she got the call from the police. They had found their shared car in a ditch off the side of a country highway.

Mike had been in a car accident. The police suspected he was speeding and his car spun out of control after running over a hole in the road.

It was fatal.

Sheryl didn't hear anything else after that. She dropped to the ground on her knees, letting the phone fall from her hands. She screamed and screamed until her voice couldn't make any more sound.

Jane, just 5 years old, was playing with her toys quietly when her mother got the call. Frightened by her mother's reaction to this phone call and confused, she ran up to her and tugged her arm. "Mommy, mommy, what happened? Mommy, what's wrong? Where's daddy?"

Sheryl paused, breathing heavily, and looked into her daughter's eyes, with tears down her face. *What am I going to do? How will I tell Jane, where do I go, who do I call?* Sheryl's mind started spinning. Her breathing picked up faster, and the tears came back.

With Jane now crying with her, all she could do was hold her daughter and weep.

Chapter 1:

The Nobody.

Jane was ordinary.

In just about every way, Jane saw herself as plain as they come; she had mousy brown hair to the middle of her back with an unimpressive middle part, an ordinary face, and ordinary blue eyes. Jane had crooked teeth because her mom could never afford braces. When it came to style, she was never unique, choosing instead to wear whatever she found within 5 minutes at the local thrift store. (Growing up in a small town in Texas will do that to you.)

Even in school, Jane was, well, plain. Plain Jane, her classmates called her. She was a straight-B student who would rather sit in the back of the class and hide from the teacher to avoid being noticed. Because of this, she never made real, genuine friendships growing up. Other students thought she was weird- when her father died when she was little, her classmates avoided her, because she was always so quiet and brooding. While her classmates were joining the soccer team, learning instruments, going on dates, and getting good grades, Jane stayed home and chose to zone out in front of the TV instead. Why make a huge effort at anything, when you feel... useless?

Jane was stuck in a prison of mediocrity under a cloud of low self-esteem.

~

"Honey, why don't you go make some friends?" Jane's mom, Sheryl, asked one day over dinner. They were eating a box of Hamburger Helper- Jane's least favorite.

"Mom, leave me alone."

Jane and her mom didn't get along well. When Jane's dad died, she ended up stuck with her mom by herself. Her mom worked late hours with multiple shifts, so Jane never got to spend time with her or have any classic mother-daughter experiences. In a way, Jane always blamed her mom for all of the things in her life she hated. If her mom made more money, they could stop shopping at thrift stores and buy trendy clothes. If her mom was more involved, maybe Jane wouldn't feel so awkward and weird. If her mom was there for her when she needed her when she was sad, angry, happy, or any other kind of emotion, maybe Jane wouldn't be so messed up.

If her mom didn't rush her dad out the door on that fateful day, her life would be better right now. She'd have her dad.

It was all her mother's fault.

Jane's mother sighed and went to put her plate in the sink when Jane exploded. Jane slammed her fist on the kitchen table, shaking the glasses and plates.

"You know, my life wouldn't be so bad if you had died instead of dad."

Sheryl paused briefly, then resumed putting her plate away. She didn't react to Jane's statement at all, and instead, shuffled emotionlessly to her room. Jane's insult seemed to hang in the air like a heavy, humid, dark cloud that covered Sheryl's whole body. Instead of reacting to Jane, to avoid hurting her more, Sheryl stayed in her room for the rest of the night. She seemed to do that a lot recently.

"No response? Typical. I'm out of here. I'm going to the football game. Don't wait up."

Jane stormed out of their modest house, slamming the door. She grabbed her rusty Huffy bicycle from the porch and furiously rode to her high school, rubbing anger-filled tears out of her eyes. If she couldn't find support at home, and she couldn't find it during school, maybe she would find someone to talk to at the football game. You know, visiting teams sometimes bring their own students to watch their games, so maybe she would meet someone her age, someone new, someone who understood her.

The sun was coming down right as she pulled up on her bike to the football stadium. Her brakes squeak loudly as she stops, which pulls attention to herself that she didn't quite want yet. To Jane, it felt like the entire stadium was turning around to look at her. Seeing a few snickers from the popular girls, Jane started wondering if this was a bad idea. She parked her bike under the rusty stands, feeling them shake above her as the crowd roared. Jane never really understood football, but she liked how it seemed like everyone had fun and got along. Maybe she would find someone to get along with, too.

Jane made her way to the stands, finding a nice empty spot- sitting next to someone right away would just be way too awkward, so she figured sitting alone would be best. She looked around, rubbing her ratty t-shirt between her hands nervously, hoping someone would come to talk to her.

Hannah, the popular girl in her class, was standing with her group of minions near the base of the stands and saw Jane walk in alone. Immediately, she looked Jane up and down and whispered with her friends. *Surely they're talking about me. I hate them.* Jane thought to herself. Hannah was perfect. She was tall, thin, blonde, and gorgeous. All of the boys liked her, and she was friends with all of the popular girls in their school. Unlike Jane, Hannah had gotten into college. She was going to the top college in Dallas. *Of course, she was.* Jane thought to herself.

Jane never made a big deal about it to her mom or to anyone she knew, but the fact that she didn't get into any of the colleges she applied for really bothered her. She may not have been a genius, but she wasn't a totally bad student, either. She was just mediocre enough that no college found her worthy of their student body. Jane put her head down, thinking about all of her failures and all of the things she hated about herself when she heard someone approaching her in the stands.

To her surprise, a jock she had never met from the opposing school came right up to her! Maybe this was her lucky day; maybe she would finally find a friend or a boyfriend! She gives him a crooked smile and a small wave. She had no idea who this jock was, and he didn't know her, but apparently, she wasn't even worth walking up to, much less talking to. He pauses, stares at her for a moment, and slowly lifts up a hand to point at her. Jane felt like the world was moving in slow motion: the jock pointed at her and yelled to the crowd of her classmates, "what a loser!"

If Jane thought that the brake squeals or Hannah's whispering to her friends was embarrassing, this was ten times worse. She could feel her face turn bright red as all of her classmates, one by one, turned to look at her. They all laughed at her, humiliating her, for no reason other than existing as she was.

Jane, with tears streaming down her face, ran down the stands to her bike and quickly rode home. While being with her mom right now wasn't what she wanted at all after their argument at dinner, she definitely didn't want to stay at the football game. In fact, she didn't want to go back to that school at all.

I wish I could just disappear.

When Jane got home, she threw her bike in the front yard and stormed inside, waiting to allow her sobs to become vocal until she safely entered her home. As soon as she got inside her house, she shrieked with a mixture of grief, anger, and pure sadness. *No one loves me. My life is horrible. I am worthless.* Jane stormed to her bedroom and threw herself on her bed, and with quiet, shaking sobs, she cried herself to sleep. Just as she fell asleep, she said to no one in particular, "I wish I could go somewhere where I mattered. Where I can have whatever I want. Where I have friends. Where I'll truly be *happy.*"

Instead of falling asleep, she was jerked awake by a strange, heavy pressure that she felt in her ears, almost like when she would swim too deep in the pool as a kid with her mom and dad. She ripped her eyes open and saw something she didn't even believe at first:

Jane was somehow floating in outer space.

Chapter 2:

The Flight.

Jane might not have been a straight-A student, but she wasn't dumb, either.

This can't be a dream. I'm probably just dreaming.

All around her were millions of stars, some shimmering, some fading, some growing stronger by the second. There were so many stars they lit up the otherwise dense, dark blanket of space around her. The stars felt to her like running your hand over smooth tinfoil: an almost metallic, light, electric feeling that gave a source of energy to her. The dark part of space felt like when Jane would put on a good pair of headphones and listen to music with heavy bass, wrapping up in a warm blanket, and closing her eyes. It felt like a never-ending pressure that somehow seemed to reverberate through her entire body. The space between the stars was darker than any black she had ever seen. The sight overwhelmed her.

Calm down, Jane. It must just be a nightmare.

She did what her dad always told her to do when she found herself waking up in the middle of a bad dream. "Do a body check, Janie! Wiggle your toes, then squeeze your muscles, wiggle your fingers, and feel everything around you. Open your eyes and tell yourself to wake up. It always works!" he would say to her after she woke up from a nightmare. So that is exactly what Jane did.

First, she wiggled her toes. *Okay, I felt a wiggle, good*. Next, she tensed her leg muscles and wiggled her fingers. *Perfect- everything is working*, she thought to herself, so she would probably be waking up soon! Lastly, she opened her eyes. With all her might, she yells out to the vast space before her: "WAKE. UP."

Wait.

But her eyes are already open. How could her eyes be open if she was in a dream? Jane closes and opens her eyes, blinking as fast as the stars around her were shimmering. Nothing happened. There was no rush back to her body, no sudden awakening in her bed. Nothing.

I'm not dreaming. Oh my god, this is real. Am I dead?

Jane realized that while she felt her body, she didn't actually see it. She stretched her arms in front of her to see her hands, and instead of arms and hands, she just saw light. Thinking it might just be a trick of the eyes, she looked down to see her body and to her shock, she only saw light again. Her body was gone, and replaced with it was a ball of light.

The light that had replaced her body was as bright as a star and felt warm, but not hot. It felt like the warmth of eating a fresh, hot chocolate chip cookie on a fall day after school. The color of the light was a pleasant pale yellow, darker on the edges and lighter in the center. As the light spread from her, it seemed to become thinner and thinner, like the wisps of a cloud as it blows through the sky on a breezy, summer day. As she paid more attention to her body, she noticed a pulsing sort of electrical current that was flowing through her body. It seemed to come from her chest, and like a heartbeat, spread through her entire self. The electrical current wasn't painful or concerning- somehow, she instinctively knew that it was good. It was her. With each pulse, brilliant shades of green spread around her light body, mixing delightfully with the yellow color of her light. It seemed to energize her light-body, and it gave her peace.

If I'm dead, this is a pretty nice place to be. This is me. This is my aura. I am energy.

Jane took a deep breath and settled into this feeling. She hadn't ever felt like this before. It felt so comforting, like all of her problems were over. She could finally rest. Jane wasn't a religious person, preferring to stick to a sort of apathetic agnosticism, so she had no idea what was going on. Somehow, though, a voice inside her told her these things about who she was, who we all are. *I guess that's what happens when you die.*

We are all light. We are all energy. We are all connected- people, the planet, the stars, even the depths of space.

Jane closed her eyes and sunk into what she was feeling. The warmth of her yellow aura was pleasant and comfortable, and the pulsing green was almost lulling her to sleep. Just as she was about to succumb completely to the energy, she saw a sudden white flash of light in front of her. Bigger than any planet she had ever seen erupted a giant ring of light.

The ring of light was white, blindingly white, and seemed to be made of static, like the static of a TV on the wrong input setting. In the center of the ring of light was... nothing. It was space, but not the space she was starting to get used to; there were no stars, no colors, no light. Just darkness, like the empty part of space. It was as if the ring had pushed all of the stars out of the way.

While she stared at this ring of light in a mixture of awe and fear, she found herself moving close to it without her control. In this light-body, she could not control where she was going- she tried to kick and swim away, grasping at nothing in the air. The closer she got to the ring, the more she started to feel the TV static in her light body. At first, the static felt like a green pulse. As she got closer, though, it got more and more uncomfortable.

Within seconds, her mind was screaming. The static took over her entire body, feeling like a thousand electrical shots. It was as if all of her cells were being bounced around like popcorn in the microwave, with each pinpoint of static causing unending pain. She didn't know if she was screaming out loud, or just in her mind. It didn't even matter anymore. As the static in her body grew, so did the ring of light in front of her.

She was then right in front of the ring of light, facing the dark empty nothingness in the center. In one final pull from the gravity of the ring, she was pulled through the center. She closed her eyes.

Suddenly, she felt a feeling she was convinced she'd never feel again.

Jane felt her feet on the ground.

Chapter 3:

The Happy Place.

Am I home?

Jane felt her feet strongly on the ground. She was suddenly more thankful to have feet and a body than she had ever been. The painful static that seemingly ripped her atoms apart just seconds before was gone in an instant. Her fear and panic were subsiding with every quick, shallow breath she took.

With her eyes still closed, Jane reached her hand to touch the ground. The ground was made of gravel, with rocks that seem to be almost smooth. This wasn't anything like the Texas gravel roads she knew so well.

Jane ripped her eyes open to see where she was, and at that moment, she knew her life would be changed forever.

She found herself on some kind of road. It was made of caramel-colored rocks and seemed to wind and stretch all over the land, which looked unending. It was the kind of gravel that didn't hurt your feet when walking on it barefoot. On either side of her was a dense forest of tall trees with dark-green leaves that seemed to dance in the light breeze that was flowing in this place. Within the dense forest were creatures she had never seen before; they were glowing with a mesmerizing neon light, with delicate, beautiful wings, like fairies. Jane took a quick glance at the vibrating and looming ring behind her and quickly walked forward. She didn't want to go through that experience ever again.

   Jane took a deep breath, and then one step forward. Then another. And another. The only way to go was forward, so she walked down the gravel road to see where it led. The road winded through the forest with seemingly no clear pattern or reason why.

   With each step she took, she found herself filled more and more with an unexplainable joy. Nothing prompted this joy, exactly- it was almost as if the very air she was breathing was filling her body with positivity. The white-neon glowing creatures buzzed happily around her as she walked, their wings making a pleasant sound in her ears, almost like hummingbirds. The air in the forest was warm, but not too warm; humid, but not too humid. The scent of fertile soil and flora filled the air like a calming blanket in this strange, beautiful place.

Jane still didn't know if she was dead, or in a strange new world, or just dreaming. As she contemplated this, she noticed that the forest was thinning up the road. She quickened her pace to see what was on the other side of the forest, and as she got close to the edge of the forest, her eyes were struck with the most beautiful land she had ever seen.

No longer shrouded by the dark green trees, the sun and sky seemed to glow above her. The sun now beamed down upon her skin, warming her pleasantly. It reminded her of going to Galveston with her mom as a kid; one of the few times she really had the opportunity to connect with her mom. They would sit on the sand for hours, drinking soda, and just talking. They didn't really talk to each other like that anymore.

Well, if I AM dead, I guess I'll never get to talk with her like that again.

Amongst the glowing sun were fluffy clouds that danced blissfully in the sky, seemingly unbothered and unmotivated by any outside force. The blue of the sky was deeply saturated and deep, promoting a sense of calm and peace, versus the confusion and anxiety she had felt previously while in space. This was nice. This was good.

In front of Jane, to the left of the gravel road, was the most incredible field of wildflowers she had ever seen. The land seemed to expand for miles, with rolling hills of all sizes. She recognized some of the wildflowers; there were some that were native to her Texas home, like bluebonnets, Texas thistle, Indian paintbrush, and firewheels. The familiarity brought Jane a sense of comfort and relief; if she was actually dead, this must be a good place. She soaked in the view of the brilliant blues, oranges, and reds mixed together amongst the bright green leaves and grass, feeling calmer and calmer the more she looked.

Beyond the familiar wildflowers, however, were large patches of flowers she had never seen before, not even in school or online. In fact, some of these flowers had colors she had never seen before. Instead of instilling panic or unease at the sight of something as momentous to her as a new color, it filled her with peace.

There was nothing Jane could base these new colors on; as her brain tried to wrap itself around this new concept, she was interrupted by the buzz of bees and dragonflies around her. They flew happily amongst the flowers, favoring both her familiar, Texas wildflowers as well as the new, alien ones. Life seemed good in this place.

Just past the field of wildflowers were gigantic mountains with snow-capped tips. Jane had lived in central Texas her entire life, so she had never seen mountains this big in person. The mountains towered around this place, almost like a giant wall.

Along the road was a babbling brook; it was just a few feet wide, and the water was clear. Shimmering rocks of all sizes, shapes, and colors lined the bed of the brook, glimmering in the sunlight and the flowing water. It produced a beautiful, peaceful sound, adding to the symphony of noises this nature was providing her.

She kneeled down at the edge of the brook where she stood and touched the water. Despite the warm sun, the water was cool as ice. The shock of the cold sent giggles through her. When she pulled her hand out of the water, her hand glimmered just like the rocks in the brook.

Jane looked closely at the water, noticing that there were tiny, microscopic creatures that seemed to float aimlessly in the water, just as the clouds floated aimlessly in the air. These tiny creatures had a similar neon glow to them like the flying creatures in the forest. They were unbothered by Jane's presence as if they were used to being bothered by people.

Are there other people here?

Just as the thought entered her mind, she noticed in the distance a humble white cabin. *I must not be alone. Maybe someone can tell me where I am.*

Jane stood back up and walked towards the mysterious house. The ground crunched pleasantly under her feet. Rather than shy, or anxious, or scared, like she would have been back on Earth, she was brave, calm, and curious. Whatever this place was, it seemed to almost have a sedative effect on her, as if she were unable to feel anything other than peace.

The white, wooden house had 4 creaky-looking steps that led to the modest front door. The steps were old and aged as if they had been walked on thousands of times over many years. There were sturdy railings on either side of the steps, which she grasped tightly. To her surprise, her left hand grazed something that startled her- a giant, garden spider. The spider was made of bright yellow and purple stripes, unlike any earthly spider she had ever seen. Its legs stretched out longer than her hand, and it was sitting comfortably on a giant web it had weaved between the wall of the house and the railing of the stairs. She had the sudden thought in her mind that this spider was a protector of this house. She paused before touching the doorknob, locking eyes with the spider. The spider seemed to almost bow to her, which she knew to be permission to enter. *What a strange place this is... How do I just know things? I hate spiders. Why would I randomly know that this was some kind of security guard for this house? What is this place?*

With a brave sigh, she turned the rusty doorknob and opened the door. She was determined to find answers- was she dead? Where was she?

Jane entered the house.

Chapter 4:

The House.

Before her was a large room with a tall, vaulted ceiling. The walls, floor, and ceiling were painted white and seemed weathered and worn like this house had been here for a long time. The house seemed bigger on the inside than it did on the outside, but at this point, not much more could surprise Jane about this place.

But this wasn't any ordinary house. Jane's house was like any other- filled with thrift store furniture, knick-knacks her mom had purchased at Ross and other discount stores, and all the comforts of a normal life. This house had almost no furniture, despite the size of the room.

The babbling brook that had accompanied her journey to the house seemed to wind right through the middle of the house. It separated the room in half, with the front half towards the door being empty, and the other half containing a simple park bench. The bench was placed in the middle of the room along the brook and faced a large fireplace that seemed to stretch from the floor to the ceiling.

The fireplace had no wood in it, so no one must have used it recently. *That's ok, it doesn't mean I'm alone here.* Above the fireplace were swirling flowers on vines in vibrant, spring colors. The vines almost seemed to have a life of their own, pulling and stretching slowly along the mantle of the fireplace.

To the right of the fireplace along the wall was a circular mirror, hung at eye level. Something drew her to the mirror, and Jane walked to the mirror as if in a trance. Dread filled her body as she realized she no longer had control over her movements. Something was pulling her in. Something wanted her to look into that mirror.

She stood in front of the mirror and looked at her face. Jane sighed a quiet sigh of relief, because it was just an ordinary mirror, until what she saw in front of her started to change. Suddenly, the surface of the mirror started to change- it rippled like water and seemed to be made of pure silver. As the surface of the mirror changed, Jane's mind froze in horror.

Her features slowly became distorted, changing from a neutral face to one of pure anger, hatred, and sadness. Her smile twisted into a frown that seemed too big for her face; her eyebrows furrowed, and her eyes turned completely black as if replaced with shiny, dark, obsidian. The darkness of her eyes was the same engulfing darkness she experienced on her journey to this strange world.

The sound of the birds chirping outside of the house began to fade, leaving Jane to stand there in silence. The room suddenly became dark, and she felt a burning fury rise up from within herself, like lava bubbling in a volcano that is due to erupt at any moment. Her eyes were locked on her reflection's eyes. At that moment, all she could think about were all of the awful things that had happened in her life. Her father dying, her mother emotionally abandoning her, and every single time she felt humiliated or lonely in school. She saw all of these memories flash in her mind like a strip of film that was running out of control.

Her face in the mirror then started to change. Her features began to disappear.

What was left was a grotesque featureless face of pure flesh. All that was left of Jane in the mirror were the feelings that were bubbling deep inside of her.

Anger. Fury. Sadness. Loneliness.

Horrified, she starts to hear a scream, soft at first, then rising to unbearable levels. She didn't know if she was screaming or if something else was.

With all of her energy, she worked to pull herself from the mirror, desperate to be rid of this nightmare. At the height of the scream, she finally broke free.

The room in the house returned back to its normal state, and the sounds of the birds innocently chirping outside came back.

What. Was. That.

Whatever that was, Jane never wanted to experience that ever again. The room lost any resemblance of negative energy, returning to its perfect, beautiful state. All of a sudden, another door appeared in the room, leading towards the back of the house.

Jane walked out that door, ready to get out of the house. She was disappointed that she didn't find anyone living in the house, and even more disappointed that she had no answers yet. Behind the back door of the house was a round, humble, outdoor glass table with three chairs scattered around it. The table was covered in dust, dirt, and pollen. It looked like it had not been used in a very long time.

She sat down at the table and took stock of what she did know about this place.

I know this isn't Earth. There are aliens, weird plants, but also plants I know. There's a freaky mirror inside the only building I can see. There are no other people.

Maybe this is heaven- or maybe this is hell. Maybe this is something different altogether.

Jane, lost in her thoughts, didn't notice the sound of footsteps along the gravel road until they got closer.

Chapter 5:

The Rebel.

The footsteps got louder as they moved closer to Jane, but she didn't see anyone yet. Instead of a person, she saw a blindingly bright glowing ball of light that almost seems to bounce as it floats towards her, sweetly hopping up and down with each sound of a footstep.

The air that previously smelled of fresh grass, lightly floral, and wet earth, started to smell of cookies- chocolate chip cookies that were fresh out of the oven. The smell seemed to be coming from this ball of pinkish light. The glow of the light bouncing towards Jane filled her with warmth and happiness and gave her energy.

Is this God?

The ball of light giggled. *Can it hear my thoughts?*

"Yes, silly! Yes, I can hear your thoughts, I mean, but no, I'm not a god!"

Jane's eyes snapped forward. The ball of light was now in front of her, but underneath the ball of light was a person. The glow of energy seemed to start to fade while the figure in front of her grew stronger and stronger.

The woman standing in front of her was one of the most beautiful people she had ever seen in her life, both real and imaginary. Her skin was as rich and warm as the fertile land of this strange place, and it seemed to shimmer in the sunlight. It reminded Jane of lotions with fine glitter in them that she used to wear when she was a kid.

The woman's hair was silver, long, and thick. It flowed effortlessly, as if it was floating underwater, and seemed to have a mind of its own. Within the thick strands of silver were flashes of blue that looked like lightning.

Her eyes were an intense, light blue, with streaks of dark blue around her pupils, like cracks in an iceberg in the arctic. They were kind eyes, but intense. Behind those eyes was someone who was fiercely intelligent and a person who exudes confidence.

The woman was wearing a cream dress that laid effortlessly on her body. At the bottom of her dress, which came to about her ankles, was a pretty floral pattern made of eyelets. The human-ness and normalcy of her dress against her silver and other-worldly hair almost made her look like... an alien.

Is... she an alien?

"Hah- I guess I would be an alien to you, wouldn't I!" the woman said with a big smile. She walked up to the table Jane was sitting at and pulled over one of the chairs and sat across from Jane. She rested lazily on her elbows on the tabletop, looking at Jane playfully.

"Hey, stop reading my mind! Not cool!" Jane rebutted, a smile creeping on her face. This woman, whoever she was, seemed like someone Jane could trust. "What... are you?"

"Wow, that's rude. You don't want to know my name first?" For a moment, the woman looked seriously at Jane. *Did I upset her? Is she going to eat me?*

"Oh my god, no." the woman replied, loosening up instantly. "I was just kidding! My name is Georgia. What's your name?"

"Oh, uh, sorry." Jane felt bad for thinking that. Georgia seemed like a nice enough alien. "I'm Jane."

"Nice to meet you, Jane. Where are you from?" Georgia asked excitedly. Jane was confused- wasn't this the afterlife? Jane sputtered out her reply- "Uh, Texas?"

"Cool, I've never heard of that planet! What dimension are you from?" Georgia said.

"Planet? Dimension? Texas is in the U.S., on planet Earth. What in the world are you talking about?" Jane's adrenaline started to rise. She was feeling a wave of anxiety wash over her, led by the confusion of where she was. She raised her voice, asking Georgia more and more loudly, "Where are we? What is this place? Am I dead? Is this heaven? Where are you from? What is going on?"

"Jane, relax! I'll explain everything in time. You must be new. Tell me about yourself. How long have you been here so far?" Georgia asked.

"I... don't know. I don't understand time here. Maybe a few hours, maybe a day, maybe longer? I just fell asleep and woke up in space, and then I went through some horrible portal or something, and showed up here."

"Ah, the portal... you get used to it."

"... used to it? Are you telling me you have been through that horrible thing more than once?"

Georgia looked at Jane with a small, kind smile. *This Jane girl is naive but sweet. I think I like her. I have a good feeling about her.*

"Let me tell you a little bit about myself. I'm from realm 4268B, in the 6th dimension. You know how I can read your mind?"

"Y-yeah..."

"Well, my realm exists in the place where your thoughts are. Where all thoughts are. We are called Celaians, and our people are in charge of the Records of Life."

"Records of Life? Like a music record? Are you guys musicians?"

She's so human. It's adorable.

"No, goofball! Records, like books. Every single thought, feeling, dream, passion, action, death, and life are collected in the central library in my realm. Every living being with a soul who has ever existed, or will exist in the future, has their own book. Their book includes not just their present life, but their past lives, too."

"How is that even possible? Those books must be huge! That can't be real." Jane couldn't believe what she was hearing. Back at home, she was agnostic and didn't care about anything outside of her small, miserable life. She had never even considered that there would be any sort of life outside of earth, much less beings like Georgia. The Book of Records was almost too much for her to understand.

"If you let me explain..." Georgia replied, with one eyebrow raised.

Struggling to keep up but hungry for more information, Jane motioned for Georgia to continue.

"If the books were purely physical, like your books on your planet in your realm, they would be too big to contain. Obviously. These books, though, are special." Georgia gazed off in thought, a twinkle coming to her eye. "These books are special. When you open your book, whatever you are meant to know at that time appears on the page in front of you. You can ask it any question you want- even about your past lives, or what you're meant to be, what your soul's mission is, or anything else! And it will just appear in front of you."

Georgia paused for a moment, lost in thought. A small smile formed on her face for just a moment until she shook it off and continued.

"My family specifically has been tasked since the dawn of time to protect the Books as the Record Keepers. Every single person in my family has had the duty of watching over the library and making sure that no harm comes to them. We are also in charge of guiding people who find themselves at our library from meditating or astral projecting."

Meditating? Astral Projecting? Jane didn't think any of that stuff was actually real.

Apparently, she had a lot to learn from Georgia. They definitely didn't talk about any of that at her public school in Texas.

"Why would people go to the library to read their Book of Records? What if they see their future, but don't like it so they change it?" Jane inquired.

"That happens all the time! The Books are fluid and always changing. No one is bound to one future- or one past. As long as they are always following their highest truth, they'll be on the right path. No matter what." Georgia could tell that this was overwhelming Jane, so she decided to change the subject.

"My father is currently in charge of the Records. It is time to be passed down to me, for me to take over. I even saw it in my own Book." Georgia squirmed a little.

"Is that a bad thing? You seemed so happy talking about it before!" Jane asked.

The shimmer in Georgia's eyes started to dampen. She sighed. "The Records are part of me, part of my destiny. My destiny has been part of a bigger plan for millennia. I don't know who's in charge of this plan, but I have a lot of pressure to see it through. My father, you see, he used to be loving, fun, and silly."

"Like you?" Jane interrupted.

"Yes, like me," Georgia replied with a sort of somber chuckle.

"But once he took over the job, he... lost his shine. He is emotionless and stoic and doesn't spend time with me anymore. He hardly even recognizes me. That scares me." Georgia looked down at her hands and twisted her hair between her fingers.

"I don't want that to happen to me. I love living. I love having fun. While my Book of Records showed me taking over my father's position, it showed me something else, too. I saw myself here, in this place, forever. Living life however I want in pure happiness. Why wouldn't I want that?"

"I... I don't blame you," Jane stammered. This was some heavy stuff. Suddenly, all those problems back on Earth that Jane thought were so bad didn't seem quite as awful.

"So I decided to run away from my life at home and come here, so I could live my life however I want to with no one to tell me what to do. One day, my portal showed up when I was sleeping. I thought it would be more... ceremonious than it was. I guess that's just a product of my upbringing- father treats everything so seriously that I thought the portal to the Happy Place would be the same."

Jane leaned forward on the dusty glass table. "The Happy Place? Is that what this place is called?"

"Oh, did you not know? I figured you came here on purpose, too." Georgia looked confused- she had never heard of someone going to the Happy Place and not knowing what it was.

"No... I was sleeping, just like you... I... I had a bad day. A really bad day. I fell asleep, and then I found myself in space. I thought I was dead! And this giant ring-"

"Portal," Georgia interrupted.

"Yes, portal- this giant portal showed up in front of me and dragged me in. It hurt so bad."

Jane slouched her shoulders, looking down at her twiddling thumbs. It wasn't a happy memory.

"I know that feeling all too well. But trust me, this place is worth it." Georgia put a hand on Jane's shoulder. Her hand felt warm and loving. Jane instinctively smiled at Georgia's act of kindness.

"So, what is the Happy Place, then?"

Georgia paused for a moment before answering. She looked around, taking in all the beautiful and perfect things around her. She closed her eyes, feeling the warm sunshine on her skin. In the distance, birds chirped- birds from realms across the entire universe. She recognized some bird calls from times when she had read the Book of Records of other souls, those whose souls were to incarnate as birds, but there were some bird calls she didn't recognize. She hoped to learn them all one day.

A light breeze blew through the Happy Place, allowing the trees in the forest to dance. She could feel the tree's joy radiating from the forest for the opportunity to dance.

"The Happy Place is a special planet in a realm that isn't really understood yet. You can't just come here. You have to be meant to come here. Even the people who have come to the Happy Place and returned to their own realms don't really understand this place. But what they do know is that this place is literal perfection.

"In the Happy Place, life is perfect. Nothing bad ever happens here- all of the creatures who live here, all of the plants, the air, the ground, the sky, the sun- all of it is made of pure energy. Pure love. Pure happiness.

"You know that feeling of joy you've had? That's the mystery of the Happy Place. It alters your aura and your energy and changes you. It makes you a happier and better person. The Happy Place intersects with your lower vibrational self and your highest self, combining it together to create pure happiness." Georgia paused for a moment, scanning Jane's face for a sign of understanding.

"Aura? Lower vibrational self? Highest self? This is all too much." Growing up in central Texas, Jane had never been exposed to this kind of hokey-pokey, as her mom would have called it. None of it made sense to her.

Sitting up taller, Georgia explained, "Your aura is the residual energy that is you. You were probably a ball of light before you went through the portal, right?"

"Y-yes! How did you know?" Jane stuttered.

"Because we are all light and energy! You can't be in your human body in space, duh. Your soul was protected by its aura in space. What color were you?"

Jane had a hard time believing everything that Georgia was telling her, but nothing made much sense in this place so far. "Yellow, I think. Yellow and green."

Georgia brightened up. "Yellow is one of the best colors to have! You're so lucky! You must be really confident, outgoing, and hopeful! And green, too? Wow, so not only are you inspirational and a leader but you must have a lot of love in your life, too!"

At this, Jane snorted. She almost felt like Georgia was mocking her. Jane was none of those things, and in fact, she was the opposite of all of those things. *How could my aura really be yellow and green?*

"Don't worry, sometimes your aura shows you not who you are in the moment but who you're meant to be." Georgia winked at Jane.

"Well... okay, if all of this is real, what's your aura color?" Jane asked.

"Mine's magenta! It means I'm outgoing, creative, and a non-conformist. That means I don't like to follow the rules," Georgia smirked.

Jane tried not to roll her eyes. She never would have been friends with someone like Georgia in school. "Okay, but I have one more question- what are we supposed to do here?" she asked.

"I thought you'd never ask!" Georgia jumped up from her seat and stood a few feet away from the table. "Watch this."

Suddenly, a glowing, strange, ice cream cone appeared in Georgia's hand.

"How... how did you... how..." Jane choked out. She couldn't believe her eyes.

"This is the coolest thing about the Happy Place. When you're here, you can manifest anything you want, instantly." Georgia paused to lick her ice cream. "Here, you try! All you have to do is picture what you want in your mind and imagine how you'll feel when you have it."

"How do I do that?"

Georgia huffed impatiently. "Think about your favorite food. Mine is this- it's ice cream made from lerden, my favorite fruit on my planet! Ice cream comes from your realm, right?" Jane stared blankly. "Anyway- what is your favorite food?"

Jane thought about it for a moment. The image of eating breakfast tacos from Taco Cabana with her dad as a young child filled her mind. A happy memory. As she thought of this memory, the breeze in the Happy Place blew a little stronger.

Georgia noticed the wind and smiled. "Ah, you must have a happy memory! That's awesome. What is it?"

"Oh, um, eating breakfast tacos from Taco Cabana with my dad."

"How would you feel if you could eat those tacos again, right now?"

Jane knew how she would feel. She would feel loved and cared for. Her stomach would ache from all of the laughter from her dad's jokes while they ate the tacos in his truck in the parking lot.

"Look down."

Jane looked down in her hands and was shocked to find two breakfast tacos wrapped in foil, just like it should be. They felt solid in her hands, assuring her that they were real. Slowly, she opened the foil to find perfect breakfast tacos, with steam coming from them. She ate hungrily and found herself filled with pure joy and happiness.

"Isn't it awesome?" Georgia continued to lick her ice cream.

Jane wondered what else she could manifest in the Happy Place. Her life felt so horrible back at home, and this was exactly what she had been hoping for: a place where she could have whenever she wanted, whenever she wanted it. Was this the answer to all of her problems?

Jane thought about it. "Can I manifest other things, too? Not just food, but stuff?"

"Of course! Try it!"

Jane considered carefully what she would manifest next. She had always wanted to learn how to ride a bike, but after her father died, her mom never seemed to have the time or care enough to teach her how to ride a bike. It was one of the things that her classmates used to ruthlessly make fun of her for. Now that she was 17, she felt like she was too old to learn how to ride a bike. But in this place, she didn't have to *learn*. She could just... know how to do it.

But first, she needed a bike.

"I'll manifest a bike!" Jane squeezed her eyes shut and thought hard. Since she had never owned or ridden a bike before, she didn't exactly know what they looked like. She tried to remember what they looked like from watching the neighborhood kids ride around on the streets in front of their houses. It was a long time since she had seen anyone ride a bike.

"Okay, Jane, you have the image in your mind? Now think of how you will feel when you ride the bike," Georgia prompted.

Jane, pleased with her image of a bicycle she held on to in her mind, focused on the feeling of riding a bike. Since she had never done it before, she thought about what it might feel like- freeing, thrilling, and fun, with the wind blowing in her hair, her heart beating fast to keep up with the pumping of her legs on the pedals. She imagined what the handlebars would feel like under her hands- kind of rough, but comfortable and wide on the handlebars. The bike would be easy to ride, and she would instinctively know how to ride it. *Okay, I think I have the feeling.*

Reading her mind, Georgia replied out loud, "Perfect. It should be right in front of you!"

Jane opened her eyes and snorted when she saw what was in front of her. Instead of a bike was a complete mess of metal, rubber, and bike parts- it looked like a child's cartoon rendering of what they thought a bike looked like without actually having ever seen one.

Jane and Georgia looked at each other, silent for a moment, and burst out laughing together, falling on the ground and holding their bellies.

Catching her breath, Georgia finally says, "Apparently you need to know what something looks like before manifesting it here!"

Jane sat up, wiping tears from her eyes from their laugh attack. "Okay, but now I know how to ride a bike. I already manifested that. What am I supposed to do with this knowledge, now?"

"I guess if you ever come across an already-real bike in the future, you'll know what to do!" Georgia replied.

~

Jane and Georgia spent the rest of the afternoon practicing their manifesting, this time with things they knew well. After a moment of pause, Jane turned inwardly. She was having so much fun in the Happy Place creating anything she wanted with her new friend from a strange planet, but she thought about her home on Earth. "Hey, Georgia?" She asked timidly.

"Yeah, what's up?"

"Can you manifest money here? I didn't really have money growing up, and I've always wanted it."

"I mean, I suppose so- I don't know what you'd need it for, but if it makes you feel better, sure." Georgia shrugged and turned away, playing with some glowing blue flowers in her hand.

Jane closed her eyes and imagined a stack of 100 dollar bills in her mind. She pictured what each bill would feel like in her hands as she sifted through the pile- it would feel like rough slips of paper, slightly dirty on her hands. She imagined the smell- like a mixture of copper and sour dirt. The color of the bills was a faded, sage green, and seemed muted in the empty, black background of her mind.

Next, Jane moved on to imagining how she would feel with unlimited cash. She never got to have this feeling when she was on Earth, but she absolutely knew how she *would* feel if she had it.

Jane thought of the feeling of pure prosperity and the feeling of being fully comfortable and at ease in life. There were so many times as a child after her dad died that she wished she had this feeling. Life wasn't easy for her and her mom. They struggled with money. Her mom had to work two jobs for as long as Jane could remember, and despite working seemingly all day and all night, they never had enough. Bills would go unpaid, lights would be turned off, and there would often be times where Jane and her mom had to go without dinner.

Growing up, Jane resented her mom for their living situation. She felt like if her mom had worked a little harder, or done a little more, they would be happier. But it just wasn't enough.

Going through school wearing torn and stinky thrift store clothes made Jane stick out like a sore thumb. Everyone avoided her because she smelled like a musty thrift store and her clothes never quite fit right. They thought she was weird and never let her fit in. As a kid, Jane would cry in the mornings before school, begging not to go. She couldn't handle the constant bullying from her peers in school. Of course, her mom would be running out the door to go to work and never listened to how Jane felt. Jane hated her mom.

"Woah, what's going on?" Georgia yelled, breaking Jane's concentration. Jane was concentrating so hard on manifesting money that she didn't even notice what was going on around her.

The previously fluffy and happy clouds in the bright blue sky were turning dark, and growing larger. The air seemed to get thicker, and it felt like there was electricity in the air. The clouds blocked out the bright sun, shrouding Jane and Georgia in darkness. Suddenly, a loud crack of thunder and lightning broke through the sky, sending sparks of electricity through the Happy Place. The bugs and creatures of the Happy Place ran for shelter.

"What were you thinking about just now? Why is this happening?" Georgia yelled over the thunder.

"I was just... I was thinking about how I'd feel if I had money, and then I was thinking about how I wished I had money when I was a kid, on earth, and..." Jane trailed off. *I caused this. I thought about bad things and bad things happened here, in this place. Wow, did I really do that?*

"Yes, you did! Now turn it off!" Georgia shouted.

"How?!" Jane yelled back.

"Think of something positive!"

Jane closed her eyes and thought of the first happy thing she could think of- the flowers she saw in the fields of the Happy Place. She imagined the flowers in all of their beauty: the

Texas wildflowers waving lightly in the wind, seemingly dancing to an unheard song sung by the wind. The flowers made her think of her home in Texas, with the warm, dry heat beating on her skin, warming not just her body but her soul. She then thought of the foreign flowers and their strange new colors she had never seen before. She felt the wonder and awe she had felt when she first saw them.

The thunder and lightning had ceased, and slowly, the clouds were growing smaller and moving apart. They returned to their previously bright and fluffy state, flowing innocently in the sky. It was as if nothing had even happened.

Georgia realized she had been holding her breath and let out a big sigh. "You have to be careful."

"I didn't know I could do that," Jane whispered quietly.

"Anyone who is in the Happy Place can do it. You can manifest physical things just by thinking and feeling them, why wouldn't you be able to manifest your emotions, too?"

Georgia responded. "You create your own reality here. When you focus on negative energy and negative emotions, you create them in the physical world."

"Well, how am I supposed to just ignore my emotions? I can't help what I'm feeling!" Jane said desperately.

"You don't ignore your emotions, weirdo! You notice them, accept them, and move on. See your feelings from the view of an outsider; recognize that you're feeling that emotion, whether it's anger, jealousy, sadness, or something else. Tell yourself that you are allowed to have this emotion. Notice what it feels like in your body and in your mind: what do you physically feel? What memories does the emotion bring up? Consider these things while always maintaining an outsider's perspective. Then, let yourself let it go. The feeling isn't gone forever, that's impossible- but what you've done is found the source of the feeling, felt it, and released it from your mind. If you hold on to it, it will fester inside you like a rotten snronglin in your stomach." Georgia wrinkled her nose at the image of a rotten snronglin.

"Rotten what? Never mind." Jane shook her head. "How do you know all of this?"

"Remember how I come from the 6th dimension, where thoughts lie? This is something we're taught from the time we are little kids. Are you not taught this on earth?" Georgia asked curiously.

"No... not at all," Jane replied.

"You are the creator of your own universe, Jane. Anything you focus your intention on becomes your reality in your physical experience. When you focus on the bad things, bad things come to you. When you focus on the good things, good things come to you. Remember that, Jane." Georgia took Jane's hands in her own in an effort to reassure her. Jane smiled.

"Thanks. I'll try to remember that."

"Hey, let's change the subject; what were you thinking about to get rid of the storm? I want to know more about that!" Georgia asked.

"Actually, I was thinking about the flowers here in this place. There were flowers from my home state of Texas and weird flowers with colors that I have never seen before. It's so beautiful how something so normal and something so... strange can combine to create something as gorgeous as the wildflower fields here."

"Oh, so those weird blue and red and orange flowers are from your homeworld? Cool! The other ones come from my home; they're average to me, but at least they remind me of home. I was wondering what those other flowers were!" Georgia laughed.

Jane and Georgia spent hours talking to each other about the different flora and fauna from each other's homes, both amazed at what the other was describing. They manifested cups of coffee and tea from their homeworlds, and basked in the warm heat from the sun.

If the rest of their lives was this, that would be perfectly ok. They had found friends in each other, and they felt like nothing could go wrong. The two manifested comfortable beds that sat on the top of a hill, so they could fall asleep watching the sun set on the Happy Place. The sound of crickets chirping lulled Jane and Georgia to the most restful and peaceful sleep either of them had ever felt. Life was good.

The next morning, however, while walking down from the hill, they found a new flower in the wildflower field: a large, white, velvety flower with petals as big as their faces. Neither of them recognized it.

Chapter 6:

The Helper.

"What do you think this means?"

Jane and Georgia were trying to figure out the sudden presence of this new flower. "Maybe it's just something I... don't know from Earth?" Jane wondered. "Nope. Doesn't work like that here. The flora and fauna that you recognize from your home planet are all things you've seen before. Same goes for me. The Happy Place can't manifest things you don't know," Georgia responded.

"Is it possible... I mean... could someone else be here?" Jane whispered.

Almost on cue, a bright beam of white light shined through the blissful clouds in the center of the forest.

The two looked at each other and then at the edge of the forest, anxiously wondering who, or what, had just entered their perfect oasis.

The dense, dark green plants and leaves of the first rustled as the visitor came through. Just as Jane and Georgia had been when they first arrived, this visitor was a ball of light: they were their pure aura and energy form. The color of this being was white, with light blue on the edges.

"Woah. I've never seen a white aura before..." Georgia said, her face stuck in a state of awe.

The being glowed through the branches of the forest as it got closer and closer. With the first step out of the forest, the being slowly shed its aura form and appeared in a body. The being looked like... well, like a human. *Could this be someone from Earth?* Jane thought to herself.

"That's no human, but I don't know what it is..." Georgia replied out loud.

The being that stood at the edge of the forest was a man. Or, it looked like a man. It was the most handsome man Jane had ever seen; he was perfect. He had blonde, short hair that laid in delightful loose curls at the top of his head. His blonde hair seemed to glow, with streaks of gold, white, and yellow.

The man's eyes were a warm, comforting hazel-brown. They reminded Jane of sweet, warm peanut brittle like she used to buy at the Texas State Fair every year. Swirling patterns of deep brown as rich as the bark of an ancient tree complimented the hazel of his eyes, adding a sense of antiquity and mystery to the visitor.

He was wearing a pure white robe that almost seemed to be made of clouds itself; the fabric the robe was made of oscillated in the light breeze, mesmerizing her as she gazed upon it. Barefoot, he didn't react to the loose gravel on the road as he walked as if he was gliding. Beneath his feet were tiny flashes of light, shimmering every time he lifted his feet.

Jane looked over at Georgia, whose eyes were locked on the man. "I... Who is he? He's... beautiful..." Georgia sputtered out. Surprised by Georgia's smittenness with the man, Jane giggled, and composing herself, yelled out to the man. "Who are you? What are you doing here?" she shouted, with just 50 feet of wildflowers separating the man from them.

The man smiled at Jane and Georgia. *Wow... that's not what I expected from his smile...* Jane thought to herself. Despite the outer physical perfection of the man, he had crooked teeth and a wonky smile.

The three met at the brook that lined the gravel road, and the man offered for them to sit with him, dipping their feet in the water. Jane and Georgia nodded, unable to speak, either from nervousness or just honest curiosity about this new being in the Happy Place.

"My name is James. I come with goodwill and love. What are your names?" he asked them. When he spoke, his voice felt like velvety butter to their ears.

"Georgia, nice to meet you! This is Jane. What... what are you?" Georgia said.

James responded, "I'm an angel. I was sent here on a mission from the council, but I do not know what the mission is yet. It is my duty to figure out what my mission is and complete it, so that I may return to the council to be given my next mission."

"Mission? Like Mission Impossible? Wait. ANGEL?! Like from the bible?" Jane asked, shouting a little from disbelief.

"I don't know what Mission Impossible is, and no, not like the bible. I am a being from the 9th dimension. All angels are given tasks to travel across the universe and assist beings when they need help ascending towards their highest selves. We visit them, mostly unseen but sometimes physically, and set things in motion in their lives to assist them. Then we leave, and help others, according to our missions."

"Who is the council? Is it like the leaders of your world? My father is a leader in my world!" Georgia interjected excitedly.

Georgia seems really excited to talk to this... angel... or whatever he is. I hope this doesn't mean she's going to ditch me for him, Jane thought to herself.

"Oh, shut up, Jane. Obviously, I'm never leaving you!" Georgia said out loud while playfully punching Jane's shoulder.

James looked at Georgia, and then Jane, confused at what was going on.

"Oh, I can read thoughts," Georgia said casually. "Continue! So who is the council?"

After a moment, James continued. "We do not know who the council is. We don't see them; when it is time for angels to receive their mission, they enter the Hall of the Council, stand in the center of the atrium, and hear a voice tell us where we are going. Most of the time, we are told exactly who we are to help and how to help them. Sometimes, though, we are not told anything. For me, this was one of those times. I was sent down a portal that opened underneath me on the floor, and through great pain, found myself here." James paused for a moment, thinking about the experience of going through the portal.

"So… it hurt for you guys, too?" Jane asked with a quiet voice. She didn't like thinking about that experience and was worried that dwelling on it would make the weather bad in the Happy Place again.

"Yes," James replied matter-of-factly.

"It hurts for everyone. I don't know why. Everyone I've ever heard that came here and went back home described it like they were being pulled apart and put back together a million times in one second." Georgia responded softly.

The trio sat in silence for a couple of seconds, contemplating their own experiences coming here.

It was Georgia who ended up breaking the silence. "Okay, so you're an angel, and you were sent here on a mission! Cool. So, who are you here to help, me, or ol' Janie here?"

Jane smiled out of the corner of her mouth at the nickname "Janie." It was what her dad used to call her.

"I do not know. I will find out, however." James replied stoically.

Wow, this guy is stiff. He needs to loosen up... Georgia thought to herself. "Do you know about this place and all of the amazing things about it?" Georgia asked, her voice getting louder with excitement with each word. "You can manifest anything you want here! This place is like magic. You can do, have, and be anything you want!" she practically yelled.

"That sounds acceptable, but I have no interest in this. I am here on a mission and must fulfill my duty. I am not here for fun and games." James straightened up a bit, confirming his rigidity.

Georgia straightened up as well, copying his movements. Jane started feeling the same way she did at the football game, before all of this. She felt like she was being pushed out and that she was eventually going to be alone, with everyone around her talking to each other and excluding her. This was not a happy feeling, which was odd, being in the Happy Place and all.

The wind started picking up around her as her feelings grew. Georgia noticed it and brought Jane in for a hug. "I've got you." She said to Jane.

The wind died down.

Jane felt better after Georgia's hug. She turned to James. "Can you tell us some stories from your angel adventures, or whatever you would call it?" Jane asked.

"Yes. I cannot tell you all of them, but I can tell you of my most recent mission." James responded. "But first, I need something to drink and eat. And a place to sit."

The trio moved to the outdoor table and chairs by the white wooden house, and as they sat down, Georgia effortlessly manifested a plate of cut-up apples and peanut butter accompanied by an iced latte for Jane, and a glass of water with a plate of what looked like a white coconut macaroon. For herself, Georgia had manifested a glowing pink liquid in a glass with a plate filled with a roasted vegetable that seemed to be changing colors.

Jane and James looked at each other, then at Georgia. "Hey, it helps to be able to read your minds!" She said to them. The three laughed together.

"I'll begin my account of my last mission." James leaned forward.

~

"The child lived on a moon called Europa. He was only sixteen years old but was already rotten from the life he had lived. He was born into a wealthy family and was given all of his desires from a very early age. You see, Europans are kind, intelligent, and giving beings, but being given everything made them cruel, thankless, and unforgiving.

His parents would bring him anything he wanted at his very call, and he never once thanked them. Caretakers would cringe when going near the boy, because of his damaged soul. He would spend his time yelling at the people around him, tearing them down, humiliating them, and trying to bring the people around him to his rotten level. To those on the outside, they saw a fortunate, abundant boy who had many blessings in his life. What the universe saw was quite different: he was a spoiled, sad, and mean boy.

The council had told me that they were worried for his higher self, who was fading with each passing day. It was my duty to save this boy, and the only way I could do it was to introduce hardship in his life.

The boy did not see me or notice me in any way. I stayed behind him at all times, monitoring his aura and manipulating his environment to make sure not *everything* was perfect. At first, it was little things- his favorite frozen treats would melt on his hand. The temperature of his room would be slightly warm or cold for his liking. Small things like that. But when I saw that he was not changing and was more negative and horrid than ever, I had to do what I dislike doing: I brought him true hardship by taking away his family.

You might be thinking that I killed his family, but no. Angels cannot kill. Instead, I helped his family realize that they were stronger than they thought and that they did not have to put up with the boy's cruelty.

Standing next to his family, I helped them stand up to the boy as they told him how he had hurt them. The boy did not react well; instead of crying and apologizing, he spewed more hatred at his family. So they did the only thing they could do:

They left him.

The boy's family gave him enough food and money to support himself alone until he was old enough to make his own way in life, and they left. The family never saw him again.

At first, the boy was angry at his family for leaving him. He would scream into his giant house every night, hoping at least someone would hear him. Unfortunately, it was only I that heard his wails.

The boy had to teach himself how to prepare his own food, do his own laundry, clean his house, pay his bills, and everything else associated with living alone. Instead of learning these things at a young age, he had spent his miserable life forcing everyone around him to do all of those tasks for him.

As time passed, he learned many lessons through his hardship. His heart slowly but surely softened, and he realized how he had taken advantage of his family when he was younger. He felt grief for opportunities and relationships lost and shame for the way he treated his family.

I knew he had learned his lesson and grown when one morning while watching the sunrise, he expressed gratitude for everything he had.

Gratitude was the driving force, the ultimate lesson that his soul needed to learn. The boy, now a man, was free from his self-imposed prison of hatred and is now living the rest of his life with pure happiness and gratitude."

~

"Wait. Wait a minute." Jane looked at him with furrowed brows. "You're an angel, but you brought BAD TIMES to him? What kind of angel are you? Are you a demon or something"

"I am just an angel, nothing more. I follow my duty. I am neither good nor bad. Plus, dear Jane, demons aren't bad like you think." James looked at her with a mischievous smile.

Jane was not satisfied, though. *Were all my problems brought to me by an angel like him? Did an angel kill my dad? Was there some lesson I was supposed to learn, or did some angel just go rogue?* Her mouth turned into a frown as her thoughts and emotions swirled.

Georgia noticed and squeezed her hand. She knew better than to talk to Jane about her feelings when she got like this because she didn't want the weather to go wonky again.

James, not noticing the interaction between the two girls, continued. "Enough about me. If my mission is to help one of you, I would certainly like to get to know both of you better. Please, tell me about yourselves." The angel offered Jane and Georgia a piece of his food, which they politely declined.

Jane and Georgia spent the rest of the night telling the newcomer about themselves- stories from their homeworlds, good memories and bad, and all about their hopes and dreams.

As the night went on, James, who was previously stiff and hardened from his sense of obligation to his mission, relaxed and had fun for the first time in a long time. He couldn't tell just yet who he was here to help, but while he figured it out, he decided that he was going to enjoy his time with his new friends.

The trio talked all night until the sun started to rise in the Happy Place. Here, they never felt tired. If they wanted to rest, they could rest, but it was for the enjoyment of resting rather than for recuperating. In the same way, they never felt hungry or the need for anything. Of course, they could manifest anything they wanted, and they did- but they did not eat for necessity, but for the beauty of the taste, the memories food held for them, and for the fun of it.

Life was perfect in the Happy Place, and the trio felt like they had found true friendship in each other. Nothing could go wrong here in the Happy Place, as long as they were together.

Chapter 7:

The Reflection.

That next morning, during a lull in conversation, James brought his attention to the white wooden house that rested on top of the brook. "I must ask- what is this house for?"

Georgia's eyes widened and she shivered. "I don't know, but I've never been there. It doesn't feel right. Why go into some creepy house when you can have whatever you want out here?"

Jane knew what was in the house, however. "I've been there. I went there on my first day here. It's just a house with a brook running through it..." she trailed off, realizing how crazy that would sound if she were back on earth. Thank goodness she wasn't back there. "There was something weird, though. A mirror."

"How is a mirror weird? What kind of mirror?" Georgia asked with her head cocked to the side.

"It... well... let's just say that I didn't see myself in the mirror. Or, I did. I'm not sure. It was weird." Jane looked down awkwardly and shuffled her feet.

She then told Georgia and James about her experience looking into the mirror.

They stood in quiet thoughtfulness after her account of her story. The birds outside of the house chirped innocently.

Georgia, never one to back down in fear, was the first to speak up. "That sounded awful, Jane, but now I'm even more curious what I would see if I looked at myself in the mirror!" She cautiously approached the front door of the house. James followed her.

"Honestly, me as well. I am curious what this magic mirror holds for me."

Georgia bravely grasped the doorknob and after just a moment of pause, opened the door as wide as it would go. The trio felt a foreign breeze coming from the open door as if there was a mysterious source of wind from within the house. Instead of gasping in fear, Georgia gasped in excitement.

"Oh, Jane, it's absolutely beautiful! This isn't creepy at all. I don't think I've ever seen a home so beautiful, and I've seen every lifetime and world in the universe!" she exclaimed.

Jane was standing behind Georgia, using her as a sort of human shield in case anything happened again in the house. When she peeked around Georgia's shoulder, she sharply inhaled and smiled.

The house looked different than when she had been in it alone. This time, it was filled with the most beautiful decorations and flowers she had ever seen. She figured that just like outside in the Happy Place, the house must grow flowers and have things from the lives of the people who visit.

"What is it?" James inquired with just a hint of glee in his voice. This was all very new to him, and he was glad to have his two new friends by his side while he explored this new world for the first time.

They stepped into the house, their footsteps echoing in the large main room.

In place of the bare park bench in the center of the room was a huge, 3-person couch with 3 fluffy pillows; The first one was large and was glowing purple and blue in intoxicating swirls. It seemed to have a life of its own. The middle pillow was smaller than the first but just as beautiful. It was made of cross stitch and had a pattern of the most beautiful sunrise on the front with a comfortable, worn-looking back made of flannel. The third pillow seemed to be made of clouds- if clouds were somehow solid. It looked like the softest pillow in the universe as if it was made of magical fibers. It was hovering pleasantly off the surface of the couch.

These pillows were here for them, they realized. This house was for them- it knew they were coming and gave something for each of them.

"How... How did it know? Did one of you do this?" James stammered. "We are able to manifest anything we want here, correct? So, did one of you manifest this for us?"

"Nope, not me," Georgia replied. They looked at Jane at the same time. "Did you, Jane? You were the only one to come into this house, so you must have!" Georgia asked.

"I didn't, I swear! When I first got here, there wasn't this couch. It was just a park bench. I don't know how this happened..." Jane replied, looking around the room.

"Well, who cares! Let's enjoy it! That's what the Happy Place is for, right?" Georgia yelled while running across the room to the couch. She skipped over the brook that ran through the middle of the house and landed squarely on her side of the couch, where her glowing pillow rested. "Wow, this is the most comfortable couch I've ever sat on! Come here, guys!"

Jane and James glanced at each other and smiled as they ran over to the couch, making sure to jump over the brook as Georgia had done. They climbed up onto their respective spots on the couch.

Jane examined her pillow, turning it from side to side, and smiled. "The flannel on the back of this pillow was from one of my dad's work shirts... he always wore flannel to the construction sites because he said it helped keep the dust off of him." She looked at the sunrise image that was carefully crocheted on the front. "I'd recognize this sunset from anywhere. It was from Christmas morning when I was ten years old when my mom had worked extra hard to make sure Santa came to visit me. She looked so proud and so happy while I opened presents."

This prompted Georgia to look closer at her pillow as well. "Woah. This is amazing! I just realized that this is the same fabric as the uniform my father and those who came before him wear while monitoring the Library." She caressed the swirling fabric as she talked. "Whenever someone in our family is promoted to be the Record Keeper, everyone in our city puts on the most amazing ceremony. Hundreds and hundreds of people who live in towns surrounding the Library come together and hold hands while making a mile-long pathway from the seashore to the Library. The new Record Keeper has to walk from the seashore to the doors of the Library to symbolize the walk all of us take through our many lifetimes as we see in the Records. While the Record Keeper walks, the people who are holding hands hum the same frequency- a healing tone that cleanses the Watcher and prepares them for their new position. It's beautiful." Georgia wiped away a single tear that had sprouted out of the corner of her eye.

"I'll always remember the look in my father's eye as he wore the swirling coat and stepped through the front doors of the Library. He was never one to show emotion, but at that moment, I swear I saw him form a hint of a smile." She sat in her memories for a moment while birds chirped cheerfully outside of a nearby window.

James took this moment of silence to glance down at his own pillow. "I don't know how this is possible, but this is made of the same fabric that my mother had used to make my childhood pillow. She filled my pillow with her aura which was pure love and light. It is the softest texture known to the universe. When I was a young angel, I never had the opportunity to experience "childhood" in the way other beings might. I was trained from birth to be a Helper. I had never known comfort and love until my mother made this pillow for me. Even after the hardest days, I would lie in my bed at night and cradle my pillow, letting its love pour through me like a crashing wave." James never broke his stare with the pillow and brushed it lovingly.

Jane was the first to put her pillow down and stand up from the couch. She looked around the house, newly decorated since the first time she had been there. *Wow,* she thought to herself, *this place really is magical. It's like it knows us from the inside out. I wonder if this is the megacenter to the Happy Place or some kind of powerhouse where the magic is or something.*

"I think you're right. This must be where everything in the Happy Place comes from. Outside of the house, we can manifest whatever we want just by thinking about it. In this house, though, we don't even have to think about it. It's like it shows us what we already want without us even realizing that we want it." Georgia replied audibly, reading Jane's mind again.

Jane nodded, distracted by the decorations all over the walls. When she had first visited the inside of the house, the walls were bare except for some of her favorite wildflowers over the fireplace. Now, the walls were filled from floor to ceiling with portraits, landscapes, and abstracts from all of their homeworlds. Some of them were minimalistic, with blank white canvas and splatters of black ink. *That must be for James.* Others were abstract and used the new colors she had seen in the flowers out in the Happy Place. *That has to be for Georgia.* Jane looked for her paintings.

To her right in the corner of the room was a portrait of someone she recognized. Her mom.

Her mom's face had a content smile, and her eyes were closed. From far away, she could make out the whole pattern of her face, but up close, it was as if it was a different painting altogether. Harsh paint strokes that seemed almost 3D dashed across her face in colors that didn't make sense; reds, blues, and greens violently interrupted her mother's face up close, but from far away, seemed normal. Perfect, even. The jagged dashes of color worked together to create something incredible. Jane had the sudden thought that this was how her mother was- a normal adult on the outside with her own fears, doubts, and losses, just like anyone else. It was not just the good things her mom did that made her who she was- it was her good and her bad that made her who she was. With this realization, Jane had a pang of guilt in her stomach. *I should have been nicer to my mom.*

Jane realized that Georgia and James behind her were oddly quiet, and turned around. The two were staring at a small mirror placed on the wall, right where Jane had seen it last. They couldn't look away.

"Is that... it?" Georgia asked, her jaw hanging slightly open.

"Yep... that's it," Jane replied quietly.

"I have to know. I have to see what it shows me." Georgia spoke as if in a trance. She let her pillow fall to the ground as she stood from the couch and walked to the mirror. As she looks at her face in the mirror, her previously blank expression turns to one of horror.

James rushes to Georgia and shakes her shoulders. "Georgia, are you alright? What do you see in the mirror?"

But Georgia didn't respond. Her mouth was slightly agape, her lip trembled as she slowly brings a hand to her face. She stroked her face, eyes locked to her own in the mirror, as she starts to panic.

In the mirror, Georgia saw a different version of herself. She saw the version of herself that she was always trying to run away from; the kind of person she was terrified to become.

A boring, passion-less, duty-bound Record Keeper.

In the mirror, this version of Georgia was old, around the same age as her father. She was wearing the uncomfortable Record Keeper's uniform, made of thick, grey, scratchy fabric that lay uncomfortably on her shoulders. Her once vibrant hair was now a subdued shade of blue-ish gray, which seemed to match her now dulled aura. In her eyes, Georgia saw sadness and regret. She saw a person who lived their life ignoring their dreams to pursue duty and obligation instead.

Georgia, a vibrant being with her magenta aura and ardor for life, was looking at a version of herself that was completely and utterly dead inside.

The future that she was escaping from.

The reason why she was in the Happy Place, to begin with.

Georgia, suddenly broken from her trance, screamed the loudest she has ever screamed in her entire life.

James, reacting to her scream, tries to tear Georgia away from the mirror. It was as if Georgia *couldn't* look away. She tried to turn her head, but her eyes were locked onto her reflection in the mirror. James used all of his strength to wrap his arms around her in an effort to move her away from the mirror.

Finally, in a last-ditch effort, James knocked Georgia to the ground, finally breaking her gaze. She collapsed into the fetal position on the floor, hugging her knees and crying, completely inconsolable.

As James was standing from the ground after knocking Georgia to the ground, he accidentally found himself looking at his own reflection in the mirror.

Jane, who was now holding Georgia, gasped, as James found himself now locked to his own reflection.

His reaction, however, was different from both Jane's and Georgia's reactions. Instead of panicking, James was frozen, as if time stopped.

His eyes began to turn red with dryness as he stood there frozen, unable to blink.

Jane looked on in horror.

In the mirror, James saw himself in the clouds of his realm, in his homeworld. He was completely alone.

The James in the mirror was a version of himself who was doomed to an eternity of loneliness, with no more missions to help people in the universe and no connections with any other beings.

No one needs his help. No one needs him.

The formerly warm and glowing whiteness of the clouds in his homeworld seemed to consume the version of himself in the mirror, slowly suffocating him; not physically, but emotionally. The version of James in the mirror then started to laugh.

This laugh was the laugh of a man gone mad. With no one to talk to, no one to help, no one to connect with, his aura darkened and shrank until it completely disappeared.

James had lived his entire life depending on the missions provided to him to help other people in the universe, which he found great pride in. James had rejected any kind of personal self-development in order to remain loyal to his missions. While on his missions, James connected with the people he helped, creating friendships and relationships along the way.

To him, the purpose of his life was these missions, and the thing that kept him going was the pride of duty and the stories he collected across the universe as he helped people.

In this mirror version of himself, however, he had none of that.

He was useless, thrown away, unneeded, and unimportant. This was James' greatest fear; that the Council would eventually be tired of him and reject him, making him spend eternity alone with no purpose.

The disturbing sound of laughter from the mirror filled James' ears, growing louder and louder until he couldn't take it anymore.

James began to scream, as the others had. He screamed so loud that his body began to tremble.

Georgia, still laying on the floor, broke out of her shock as Jane jumped up to try to pull James down to the ground. Jane couldn't pull him down on her own; she pulled and pulled at his arm to no avail.

Georgia saw her friends struggling and gathering bravery from within, she closed her eyes and pulled at James' ankles, tripping him.

This move from Georgia is what it took to break James' trance, and James fell to the floor with a loud thump, bringing Jane down with him.

The three, now on the floor together, looked at each other. They gasped for air, trying to understand what had just happened.

A while had passed where none of them spoke, and it was James to be the first to break the silence.

"I have seen this once before. A long time ago. This wretched mirror shows you your worst fear." James gulped.

"When you look in the mirror, it grabs you. With its strong grasp, it pulls you in and traps you in its gaze, forcing you to live your worst fear over and over until your mind can't take it anymore."

"Worst fear? Why did it show me my mom, though? My worst fear is snakes." Jane said quietly.

"Not your worst external fear," James replied, "but your worst fear about yourself, your life, your future, your highest self. That is your true deepest fear, the fear that drives your actions- even if you don't know it at the moment."

Jane still didn't quite understand, but looking over at Georgia, she decided to keep her confusion to herself. Georgia was significantly more pale than before the mirror, and she wanted to tend to her friend instead. Jane, still on the floor, crawled to Georgia where she sat against the wall, holding her knees and staring ahead. She held Georgia in her arms when Georgia softened significantly.

James crawled over to sit with Jane and Georgia and the three embraced each other in silence, while the quiet, humble sounds of the babbling brook inside of the house serenaded them.

Chapter 8:

The Visitor.

The trio lived in The Happy Place for another thousand years, blissfully creating their own reality every moment of every day. The horrors of the mirror were never seen again by the three friends, as it had somehow disappeared when they entered the house again the next day. Life was good in The Happy Place. Jane, Georgia, and James had everything they could ever want or need, and they planned on staying there for the rest of their days.

Time moved differently in The Happy Place. A thousand years there equaled just a few weeks on Earth, a few years on James' home realm, and a few months on Georgia's home planet. The trio didn't age while there, and never felt pain or sickness. They ate for the pleasure of eating, not for the need of it. They drank for the joy of it and slept when they wanted to dream.

The friends did a lot of exploring together to see just how far The Happy Place went. Even after a thousand years, they always discovered new areas of all kinds of climates. There was always something special for each person at each new area they discovered, whether that was a plant, animal, smell, or element from each of their homeworlds.

For Jane, she always thought of home whenever they came across a new hot and dry desert area. It reminded her of Texas and kept her somewhat grounded to her home back on Earth. Sometimes, the wind in the dust would remind her of the dust devils that would swirl around in her front yard back at home. Sometimes, the blanket of heat in the desert would remind her of Texas summers; playing in the sprinklers in the front yard and eating ice cream from an ice cream truck.

Georgia particularly enjoyed the dense forests they discovered. Her homeworld was full of rich life, mostly covered by deep and tall forests, hidden from the sun, and illuminated by the bioluminescent creatures that lived inside of it. They reminded her of her childhood when she would run through the forest chasing the glowing animals while filling the forest with the sound of her joyful giggles. When she was young, she never had to worry about her future duty as a Record Keeper. All she had to worry about was living.

James thought of his home whenever he looked to the sky on a warm, cloudy day, especially in late spring in the Happy Place. He would think of laying amongst the soft, billowing clouds of his home that would surround him with a feeling of peace, tranquility, purpose, and universal love. In his home, he didn't need much; it was just the feelings he had there that would keep him going whenever he would be on long missions. Sometimes, while in the Happy Place, James missed his home; but most of the time, he was happy to create new memories with his new friends while on this current unknown mission, living each day as it came.

No matter the weather, the terrain, the creatures or plants, or anything else, the trio had lifetimes of happy memories together in the Happy Place. Being able to manifest anything their minds thought of in an instant meant that Jane, Georgia, and James had everything they could ever want or think of, and they were able to create their own individual perfect images of a happy, perfect life. There was never a reason to go back to their homelands; even James had forgotten about his mission, delighting in his ability to create reality in front of his own eyes. Georgia had all but moved on from her expectations and duties back home, hardly letting it get to her anymore. Jane had stopped feeling angry toward her mother, angry toward her father for dying, and angry for her not-so-great life back on earth. When one can manifest your own reality, there is no need to worry about the things that bothered you in the past.

One day while Jane was walking through the bright, verdant woods near the white house, she found herself thinking about her mother.

Where she was, how she was doing, and if she missed her daughter. All of the time spent in the Happy Place gave Jane a different perspective on her previous life on Earth. She had realized that there is so much more to life than the negativity that holds you down. She used to blame her mother for her father's death and for her childhood, but now she realized that her mother was doing her best under horrible circumstances.

As her mind churned, Jane felt a twinge of guilt about the way she used to treat her mom. This didn't last long, however, because it started to feel like the image of her mom in her mind was fading. Once a vibrant and detailed thought in her mind's eye was now fading to grey, with her features blurring with every second. She struggled to remember her mom's face, and in a panic, attempted to bring back any memory of her mom. Trips to the grocery store, playing at the park as a child, watching television together- all of it was fading.

"Hey, guys?" she asked timidly that day while the trio walked along a glowing, golden trail that snaked through the trees in the woods near the white house.

"What's up?" Georgia replied. *Hmm. She's upset.* Georgia thought to herself after reading Jane's mind.

"Do you remember... your families? I... I think I'm forgetting about my life before this place. It's all grey." Jane looked down at her feet, twisting her brows.

The wind started to pick up around her in a flurry, enlivened by Jane's anxiety and worry.

Georgia put her hand on Jane's shoulder. Jane's brows unfurrowed, and the wind died down along with them. Jane let out a shaky sigh.

"To be honest, I'm having a hard time remembering my home, too." Georgia paused for a moment, struggling to remember her father, her family, her people. Birds chirped nearby, sweetly filling the empty air.

It was James who broke the silence.

"I have seen many worlds, and even more people, in my lifetime. Over time, faces blend into each other and experiences fade away. I have realized that all of us are part of the same universal energy; we are all one. I, too, am forgetting my original purpose here." He paused to collect his thoughts.

Georgia and Jane looked at him, silently urging him to continue. *He's so wise...* thought Georgia dreamily.

"Look at all that we have here," James went on to say. "There is no place in the universe like The Happy Place. We can have whatever we want and live forever, in pure bliss, joy, happiness, and... love." He glanced over at Georgia, whose eyes sparkled at that moment. "Here in The Happy Place, we are becoming part of the collective *one*, the universal consciousness. We are manifesting our perfect lives and creating a world of harmony. Live is perf--"

James was cut off by a sudden muffled scream coming from the woods behind him.

~

The trio froze in fear. In the thousands of years that they had occupied The Happy Place, they had never seen any other being besides the animals that inhabited the place.

James instinctively put his arms out to shield his two friends, cautiously turning his head toward the source of the sound. "Who are you? Do you mean harm to us?" he called out.

Instead of an audible response from the intruder, however, came another scream. This time from Georgia. The leaves beneath her crunched loudly as she collapsed to the ground, holding her head.

"STOP! STOP SHOUTING!" Georgia cried. As she writhed in pain on the ground, with her friends clueless as to what to do, the sky darkened around them. Thunder rumbled in the distance.

Some bushes, just 20 feet or so ahead of them on the path, suddenly rustled, scaring the trio again into complete silence. No one moved.

In The Happy Place, there were no predators, and there were no harmful creatures towards the trio. This was something new, and it awakened a deep fear in them, a fear that had not been felt in a very long time.

Out of the bushes came a man- his hair and skin were almost identical to Georgia's; his hair glistened as if made of shimmering silver string, and his skin reflected the earth with a deep richness, however, he seemed pale and sickly, like the ground during a drought. Instead of a creative, loving, magenta aura, this intruder was surrounded by a black void. It was as if his entire sense of existence was fading away into this void that consumed his entire body.

The man stumbled towards the trio, not making a sound. As he got closer, Jane gasped in horror. The man had no face. Features like eyes, a nose, and a mouth were replaced with smooth, blank skin.

The trio stared in horror at the man in front of them. It was a mixture of fear and curiosity that kept them from running away.

As the man got closer, Georgia spoke.

"I... can hear him. I can hear his thoughts. He can't speak out loud... he is one of my own, from my world. He wants me to tell you his story.

"His name is Aurelius. He was a celebrated Keeper of the Records hundreds of thousands of years ago… he had heard stories of this place, where we are now and wanted to find it for himself. He left his family, his home, his planet, everything he loved, in search of a place that could provide *more*.

"He searched The Records for many, many years, looking for information on this place. When he finally found a clue that would lead him to the portal, he quickly left for it and found himself here.

"He says he has been here ever since, for thousands of lifetimes, and that he found everything he ever wanted. He manifested every single thing in his life that he could ever want, but over time, it became… too much, and not enough at the same time. The same pleasure he says he found from creating his own reality turned into numbness. He couldn't find joy in anything anymore. He missed his family, his home, his life…

"Very quickly, any resemblance of happiness he felt here only turned into fear. He lost himself. He says he doesn't even remember what his mother's face looked like..."

Jane winced, eyes bulging in horror.

"That's how his face turned into this, I think," Georgia continued. "He is lost, gone forever... trapped here, without a soul or identity to guide him."

James let out a sigh and looked at the ground. He couldn't stand to look at the man; he was too horrifying to look at. James wondered if he was ashamed of looking at the man because he was also afraid of turning into him.

"He's... he's screaming again. No, stop yelling! He's warning us... he says to get out of here before it's too late. No, stop!"

The faceless man suddenly turned his head towards a nearby small waterfall in the distance, just off the forest walking path they were standing on. He ran towards the tall rocky cliff, standing atop the waterfall.

"NO!" Georgia screamed in horror. Only she knew what was going to happen next- she could hear his moans and cries in her mind as he made his final move.

The faceless man jumped off the cliff. He stopped moving.

The looming clouds and thunder suddenly increased tenfold, and a damaging storm rained down on them in that instant.

At this time, The Happy Place was not so happy anymore. The trio worried that they would one day become like this man who killed himself to escape this place; would it be possible for them to lose themselves, too?

Jane tried thinking of her mother. She was losing the memory of her mother, but not just her mother's face; her mother's voice, childhood memories, and worst of all- memories of her father from when she was young before he died. Jane started panicking, which led to the storm increasing in size until a bolt of lightning struck a nearby tree, knocking a branch down onto the trio.

Jane's eyes closed as her head hit the ground, and the last thing she saw as she slipped away was the storm dying down and the sun coming out of the trees.

She let herself succumb to the darkness.

Chapter 9:

The Mother.

Sheryl woke up and noticed that her daughter hadn't woken up yet to get to school. She was going to be late for work and didn't want to deal with the hassle of taking her to school herself and missing work.

"Jane, wake up!" she yelled from across the house. Jane didn't make a sound.

"Jane...? You ok?" she shouted, this time a little more gently. A sense of worry crept onto her face. She tentatively walked towards her daughter's room to check on her.

"Jane? Jane, get up. It's time to wake up, now. I know you're embarrassed about what happened at the football game, but you still have to get up. You can't stay in bed all day." She paused for a moment to give her daughter a chance to respond. When no response came, she spoke again, this time raising her voice. "I'm going to be late for work. You know I can't miss another shift. You have to get up, now!"

But Jane didn't get up. Her mother walked over to her and shook her, first softly and then roughly, all to no avail.

Sheryl immediately called an ambulance to take her to the hospital. Why wouldn't her daughter wake up?! Jane was breathing still, but completely... gone.

At the hospital, her doctors were completely stumped. After hours of tests, the attending doctor walked into their hospital room.

"Your daughter seems to have fallen into a coma. We checked every possible reason why this might have happened, and she is completely healthy. We... can't figure out why she won't wake up." The doctor paused, allowing Sheryl to ask any questions or offer some kind of response.

Instead of speaking, Sheryl was thinking about how she didn't want to lose Jane. She had already lost her husband, she can't lose her daughter, too! The only sound that filled the silence was the beeping and whirring of the machines attached to Jane in her hospital bed.

The doctor continued. "I'm so sorry, ma'am. All we can do is continue to monitor her. Please let us know if you have any questions." The doctor lowered his head and walked out of the room.

As soon as the door clicked shut, Sheryl collapsed on Jane, shaking with silent sobs.

She was reminded of when she arrived at the car accident scene where her husband died when she had shaken him, trying to wake him up just as she did with Jane that morning. She shuddered. Her mind, consumed with grief and panic, went blank in her mind.

While the doctors didn't know what had caused her coma, Sheryl blamed herself. If she just cared more about Jane's problems, or if she worked less, or if she worked *more*, maybe her daughter would still be awake.

Sheryl lifted her head to look at Jane's beautiful face. Her perfect daughter, who worried so much and struggled so much in life.

She hoped that Jane would open her eyes at this moment and wake up, but instead, only her chest moved up and down as she breathed.

Sheryl laid her head back down and soaked the blanket with her tears.

Please wake up. Please come home. Please don't leave me.

Chapter 10:

The Fade.

Back in the Happy Place, Jane, Georgia, and James were waking up. The storm had knocked a branch on them, and when all three fell to the ground, they had hit their heads and passed out.

"What... what happened?" Jane asked, tentatively.

"Looks like we passed out. We're ok though- how could we not be, in the happiest place in the universe?" James responded, immediately cheering up.

"Yeah! You're right! Let's get up and go have some fun- maybe we can go make an ocean to swim in, or a plane to fly around, or just fly without a plane!" Georgia added, immediately cheering up as she sat up on the ground.

The sudden cheeriness from James and Georgia didn't bother Jane, because she too quickly felt happy again. That's what the Happy Place did to you; you could never stay unhappy for too long.

They stood up and continued on their way.

~

For another 50,000 years, the trio lived in pure bliss in the Happy Place. They eventually forgot about the strange, faceless man- they forgot most things that happened to them, but this didn't bother them. Each day was a new day with endless possibilities. In the Happy Place, they didn't age, get ill, or seriously harm themselves. Because they were able to manifest anything their minds could think of, they could remain themselves on the outside with no visual change.

In the Happy Place, they could be whoever they wanted to be. There was no such thing as failure to them. Every single project or idea they had came to perfect fruition.

One thing that *did* change in the Happy Place, however, was the house. The fear they felt from their experiences with the mirror in the house had completely gone away, leaving their minds with many of their other memories from the Happy Place. The house, first having just a single park bench placed in the middle of the room, was expanding. There were now three bedrooms, one for each of the friends, which were intensely customized by each of them.

The main room of the house no longer had blank, white walls. The walls were covered floor-to-ceiling with beautiful art that the trio created during their time in the Happy Place. Each piece of art contained little bits of each person; their favorite colors, the plants and animals of their homeworlds, their loved ones back home. Over time, however, the art on the walls seemed more convoluted. Colors swirled together and borders were confusing and unnatural.

They didn't mind.

Life in the Happy Place was perfect. Why leave? Jane felt that she finally had everything she missed out on during her childhood. Georgia had escaped her fate of duty to her family. James had finally found love and happiness through a family.

One thing the trio always avoided was their portals, which always remained. Their portals had been the way that they came to the Happy Place, and none of them wanted to risk accidentally falling back into it.

~

One bright and sunny day, Jane, Georgia, and James were walking along the path outside of the house which led to the dark green forest. It is near this forest where Jane's portal presided.

As they laughed and talked together, they carefully avoided Jane's portal. However, Jane noticed something... concerning.

"Hey, guys?" she interrupted.

"Yeah?" James replied.

"Do you think my portal... shrunk?" she asked curiously.

"I mean, maybe? Why, who cares? We'll never go through our portals again, right?" Georgia responded with a laugh.

Jane joined her with her own giggles. "I guess you're right!" she exclaimed.

With that, the matter was closed, and they went on their way, creating another perfect day out of the millions of perfect days.

~

That night while lying in bed and staring up at the ceiling, Jane thought about her shrinking portal. *I don't want to leave. I don't want to leave. But... what if I did? Would I still be able to?*

She thought about her mother. Well, she tried to.

Jane realized that she couldn't visualize her mother at all. She barely even remembered that she *had* a mother. All of her memories- gone.

She had finally lost all of her memories in the Happy Place. Jane didn't care.

She didn't need a mother in the Happy Place.

The next morning, Jane met with her two companions at the outdoor table in the garden of the house. She brought with her a warm, comforting cup of coffee. Georgia was drinking a thick, blue liquid, and James didn't have anything (as usual- "Angels don't need caffeine!" he would say). Jane recounted her realization from the night prior.

"Do you guys have any memories left?"

"Nah. I mean, I don't think so. I haven't thought about it. Why would I?" Georgia replied while gulping down her drink. *She's worrying too much,* she thought to herself after reading Jane's mind.

"That doesn't bother you?" Jane asked.

"Nope," Georgia replied cheerfully.

James nodded in agreement.

Comforted by her friends, Jane dropped the issue. They were right. It isn't a big deal. They've been there longer than most creatures in the universe live. In the Happy Place, they've learned every language from every planet and culture in the entire universe; they've mastered all scientific pursuits. They've created an entire perfect world, made just for them. Nothing could go wrong in the Happy Place.

Until it did.

~

After their talk at the outdoor table, Jane suddenly found herself standing in the middle of the house, in front of the fireplace. *How did I get here?*

It was as if she was in a daze. The world around her started swirling together, just like the paintings on the wall. She struggled to remain standing up; suddenly, something new caught her eye- a new flower above the fireplace. It was a lily.

The lily stirred something inside of Jane. She was then thrust backward, as if pulled by an unseen force, and found herself now back on Earth, in a church. Everyone was wearing all black and crying. There was an organ gently playing in the background. No one seemed to notice her or even realize she was there.

Jane walked forward towards the front of the church. At the end of the center aisle was a closed coffin covered in lilies. She slowly moved her hand towards the coffin and lifted it.

The person inside the coffin was her father. As she looked at his face, so cold, pale, and still, the world around her swirled again as she was thrust out of the church and back to the house in the Happy Place.

This time, she found herself staring at herself in the magical mirror- the mirror that had terrorized the trio so long ago, which had been put away and covered with a blanket. It now sat on a wall in the house right at Jane's eye level. *How did I get here? What's happening to me?*

The mirror locked her eyes at her reflection, just as it had done before. This time, while staring at her reflection, she didn't see anything. Instead of her eyes, nose, and mouth, was just smooth skin, just like the man in the forest. Even though she knew she should be scared at this moment, she felt nothing. Jane was as blank inside as her face. She felt no happiness, no joy, no love. She couldn't remember anything; she had no idea where she was or who she was. Even the knowledge of James and Georgia were completely gone from her mind, and replaced with... nothing.

The feeling of numbness completely consumed Jane. One moment felt like a lifetime. Just as she was giving into the void of nothingness, she found herself being thrust from the mirror, moved to a different place and time.

Where am I now?

Jane found herself atop a beautiful hill- one that she and her friends had visited many times together. The hill was covered in wildflowers of all shapes and colors, which moved sweetly in the soft wind. Jane looked around to see Georgia and James, who were staring ahead listlessly.

"Hey! How did we get here? Are you two okay?" she asked, running towards them.

"Who are you?" said Georgia, with a monotone voice. "Where am I? Who am I?"

Georgia stared ahead without blinking. A bit of drool dripped down her mouth. Her previously bright magenta aura was now completely black.

James didn't even respond, and only stared ahead. He was completely catatonic. His once glorious aura was now dull and grey.

"I... I don't know who you are. I just know I know you... or do I?" Jane stammered. She was starting to forget who they were, and more importantly, she was forgetting who *she* was.

James finally spoke. "This place is beautiful. I think I'll stay here forever."

"Me too..." Jane started to reply until something caught her eye in the distance. A dark portal; it had stars in it, and was surrounded by a glowing light. Somehow, Jane knew she had to get to it. She had forgotten why, but it was as if something deep inside of her was pulling her to it.

Jane ran down the hill towards the portal, and the closer she got to it, the more she started to remember. Not only the purpose of the portal, but her time in the Happy Place, her life on earth, her loved ones, and her own self. As the memories started flooding back, she looked at the portal with wide eyes. It was smaller than ever.

She knew that she had to get through the portal if she were ever to go home. The thought of turning into a faceless monster like the man in the forest horrified her.

In a sudden realization, Jane knew that the Happy Place was fading her and her friends. There would be a point of no return, where she would not be able to experience happiness anymore. She knew what she had to do.

Jane had to get home.

Chapter 11:

The Promise.

Back on earth, Sheryl visited her daughter in the hospital every single day after work. While Jane laid in her bed, condition unchanging, Sheryl told her stories of her childhood; fun times at the State Fair, memories with her father, and all the moments that made Sheryl smile over the years.

Sheryl hadn't felt this close to Jane in so many years; not since she was a baby. She found herself telling Jane about her days at work, opening up in a way she had never before.

One day while Sheryl laughed to Jane after sharing a funny childhood memory, Jane's doctor walked in.

"Oh, I'm so glad you're here. I have some unfortunate news." The doctor paused, as he always did, surveying Sheryl's face for her reaction. Sheryl's eyes widened with hope.

"Is my baby going to wake up soon?" she asked excitedly.

"Ma'am, I'm so sorry. Your daughter is dying. We don't know why; nothing we can find is triggering it. Her organs are shutting down, and none of our efforts to save her are working."

Sheryl closed her eyes, with tears silently streaming down her face. "How long does she have?"

"I'd say she will be gone within the week."

Sheryl wept as the doctor left the room.

"Please, baby. Please, Janie. Wake up. Wake up for me. If you come back and wake up, I promise I'll be a better mom. I'll do anything if you just wake up." Sheryl sobbed to her daughter.

Only the sound of the machines connected to her daughter coldly filled the room.

Chapter 12:

The Escape.

Back in the Happy Place, Jane found herself standing in front of her portal, which was rapidly shrinking. The Happy Place, which had felt so loving and precious to her for so long, now felt grey and uninviting. The shimmer of life in this place had been replaced by monotony. What used to be special was no longer special.

The perfection was gone.

As the world around her turned more and more grey, she stumbled to the ground, falling on her knees in front of the portal. In front of her, the portal was getting smaller by the second. Soon enough, it would be too small for her to fit through.

With each passing second as the portal shrank, so did her will to survive and her will to leave the Happy Place. Her hope was gone. It was over.

I'm going to be stuck here forever. Mom, I'm sorry.

As Jane closed her eyes for what she thought would be the last time, she heard a voice she had not heard in hundreds of thousands of years.

Her mother's voice.

It seemed to come from outside of her and inside of her simultaneously. The sound of her mother's voice made her open her eyes.

"Wake up. Wake up for me."

Her mother's voice gave her newfound energy, lifting her up out of her drudgery. Jane stood up and slowly stumbled towards her portal.

It was at this moment that her dearest friends, Georgia and James, approached her. Their faces had already started to turn blank; they were fading. The Happy Place was taking them.

"Where are you going? Stay here. Stay with us forever. This place is perfect. You can have whatever you want..." Georgia trailed off, staring at nothing in particular as she spoke to Jane. Jane's heart broke as she remembered all of the lifetimes of memories they had together. She knew that Georgia had completely forgotten her.

"You both have to come with me. You can't stay here. You'll be lost forever! This place will suck the life out of you!" Jane pleaded. She looked over at the entrance to her quickly shrinking portal.

Jane only had seconds left. It was now or never. She looked at James and Georgia with pleading eyes, begging them without words.

"Please... I can't go without you. Please..."

James and Georgia only stared ahead with dull, blank eyes, and both slowly shook their heads.

Jane took one last look at her friends and the incredible world that had hosted her for so many years. She had learned more than any one human could learn; most of all, she learned that you cannot have pure happiness without pain. There must be balance; just as the moon and the sun and night and day balance each other, you must have joy and suffering to live a truly fulfilling life; otherwise, happiness will only consume you and turn into nothing at all.

With a deep breath and tears in her eyes, Jane stepped through her portal, just as it closed shut behind her.

~

Jane was sucked through the white static of the portal, as if in a vacuum, just like when she first arrived at the Happy Place so long ago.

The portal spit Jane out into space, with nothing around her except for stars and galaxies far away, and an almost painful quiet surrounding her. Just as she had arrived, while in space, she found that she had no physical body; she was just a ball of light.

At least my aura is back to normal... she thought to herself.

Jane looked around her. *How am I supposed to get home? Where is home?*

In the silence, she thought of her time in the Happy Place. She remembered all of the incredible memories she had with her two friends, all of the things they learned together, and how much all three of them grew as people in the Happy Place. Jane also thought of her mother- *she must be so worried about me.*

Jane held the memory of her mother's voice close in her mind, letting it shower her in love and safety in the cold void of space.

I'll never see them again. Georgia, James, mom... I'm alone. Forever.

With this realization, Jane closed her eyes one last time, letting the void of space consume her completely.

As reality around her faded away, the loud sound of beeping machines startled her. She shot her eyes open and looked around.

Where am I? Am I home?

Jane looked around and saw that she was in a bright, sterile hospital room, hooked up to whirring and beeping machines. In the corner of the room was her mom, slumped over in a stiff chair. Her mom was crying.

"Mom?" Jane called out weakly.

Sheryl jumped up. "Janie? You're awake! You're awake! Oh, my baby! My little girl!" she shouted. Sheryl ran to Jane's bedside and held her hand, gazing into her eyes.

Something had changed about Jane; she seemed wiser and older somehow but remained as young as she was when she first entered the hospital. It didn't matter to Sheryl- her daughter was awake and *alive.*

"Mom, I heard you. You saved me. Your voice... it brought me out from the fade. Thank you..." Jane said quietly to her mom. She closed her eyes, letting tears fall from them, as she thought of her dear friends back in the Happy Place, who must be completely faded by now.

Sheryl didn't understand what Jane was talking about, but it didn't matter.

Jane was alive!

Chapter 13:

Epilogue.

It had been 5 years since the Happy Place.

Of course, no one had believed Jane when she told them stories from her time there. Her doctors chalked it up to dreaming during her coma- though not a single one could explain how she suddenly knew so much about the universe.

Jane had returned to her home with her mother, where they spent lots of time together during her recovery. The stories that Sheryl had told Jane while she was in her coma were re-told, this time with laughter and smiles as responses instead of the quiet beeping of the machines in the hospital.

After the Happy Place, Jane was a changed person. Before her experience, she was miserable; she thought she had nothing good in her life to be thankful for. Now, after experiencing every single happy and blissful thing in the entire universe, Jane was wiser and stronger.

She took the manifestation skills that Georgia had taught her and applied them to her life on earth. It didn't work exactly the same as it did in the Happy Place, but sure enough, one by one, her manifestations of happiness started to come true. This time, pain and suffering would sometimes accompany her manifestations.

When Jane experienced pain and suffering after not feeling it for hundreds of thousands of years, instead of wallowing in self-pity, she fully *felt* the pain. She allowed herself to completely feel all of it. Pain and suffering made the good times so much better.

~

Jane wrote a book about her experiences in the Happy Place and the lessons she learned there. At just 23 years old, she became a best-selling author and was able to retire on the money she earned from her book. After making her money, she decided to live a simple life in her hometown.

She opened a humble flower shop, biking-distance from her childhood home, where she chose to continue to live with her mother. Her flower shop reminded her of the beautiful wildflowers in the Happy Place; while her flowers could never compare to the otherworldly flora there, they brought her comfort and made her think of her two friends she lost to the Happy Place.

More than the success of her book, or her cozy flower shop, the newfound relationship with her mother brought the most happiness in her life. Whether that was manifested by Jane or came about naturally, she would never know.

~

One warm spring day while Jane was tending to some beautiful bright blue flowers in the back of her shop, she heard the ding of the bell on the front door. A new customer.

"Be right there!" she called to the front.

When Jane got to the front of the store, she stopped dead in her tracks. Her mouth dropped open in shock.

In front of her stood two very familiar people. A woman with silver and purple hair, and a man with an angelic face.

The three friends smiled at each other.

Made in the USA
Columbia, SC
03 July 2025